Printed in the United States of America

First Printing, 2017

ISBN-13: 978-1544134154

Cinnamon Cake font by Brittney Murphy Design

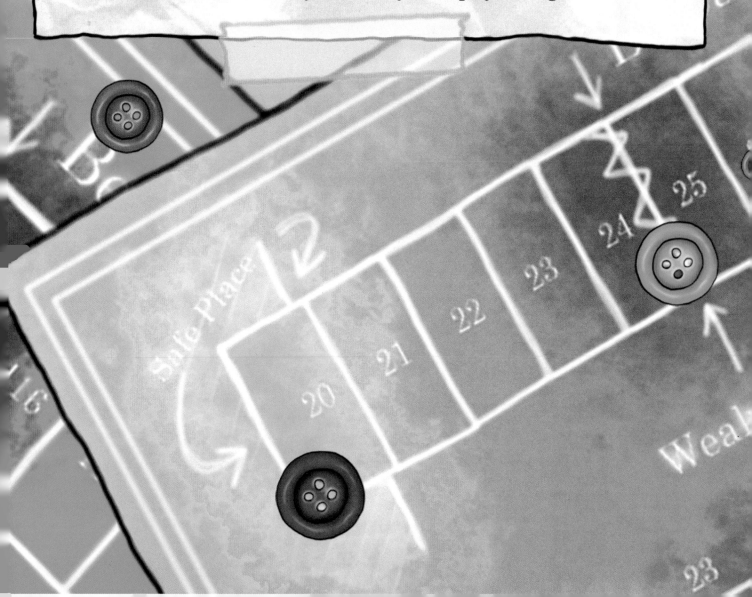

Fuzzballs!

A Rounding Adventure

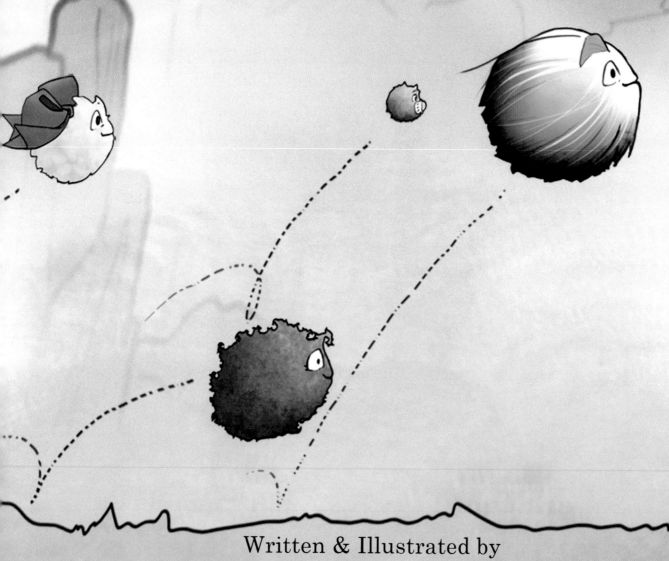

Written & Illustrated by

KA Long

Fuzzballs Hate:
- Gum
sticks in hair!
ouch!
- Fire
- WATER!!!
can't even look at!!!
I just looked at it!!!

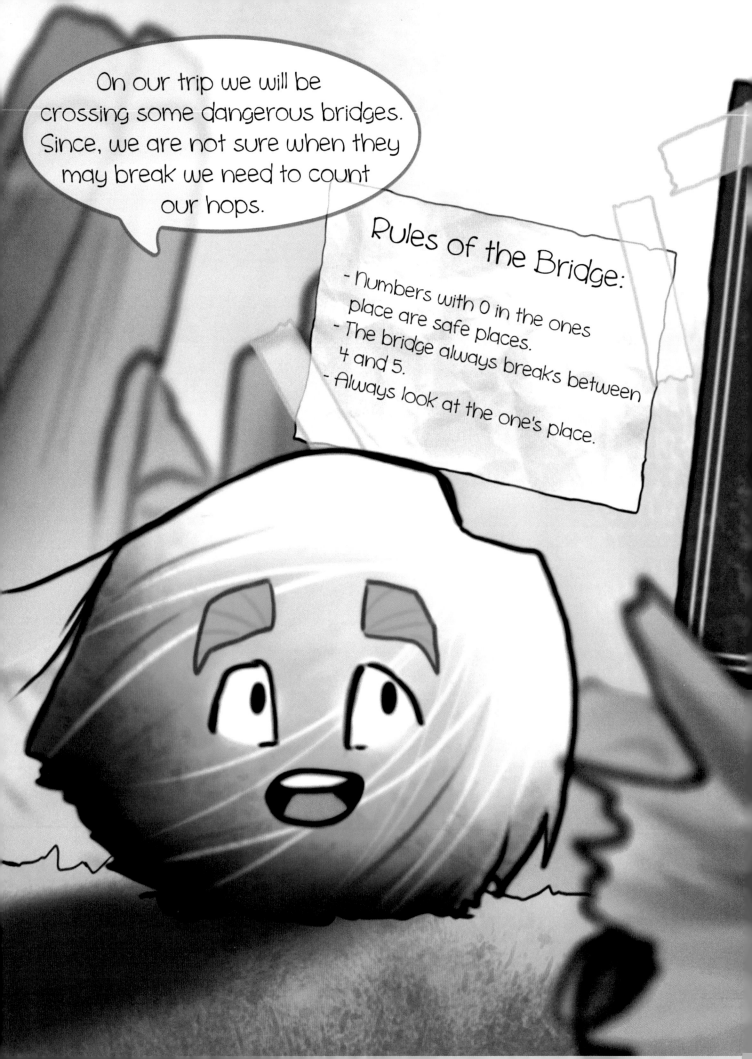

Be Careful!
0 1 2 3 4 5 6 7 8 9 10
Weakest Part
Safe Place
0 1 2 3 4 5 6 7 8 9 10
Safe Place
Plans
So if the bridge breaks, we hop to the green places.
I will stay away from the red places.

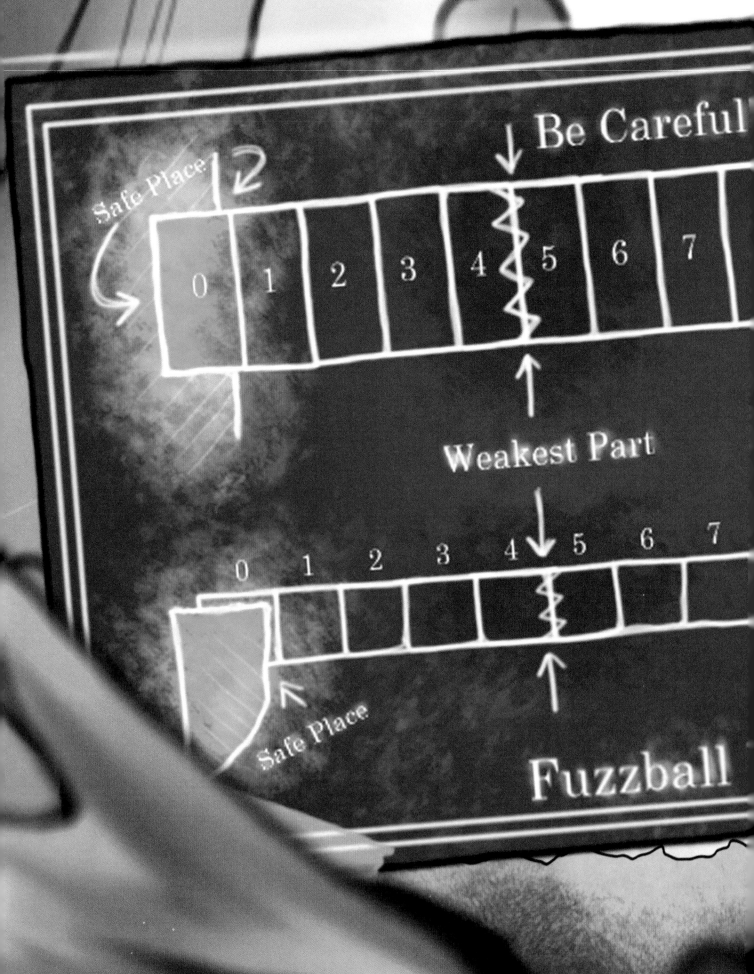

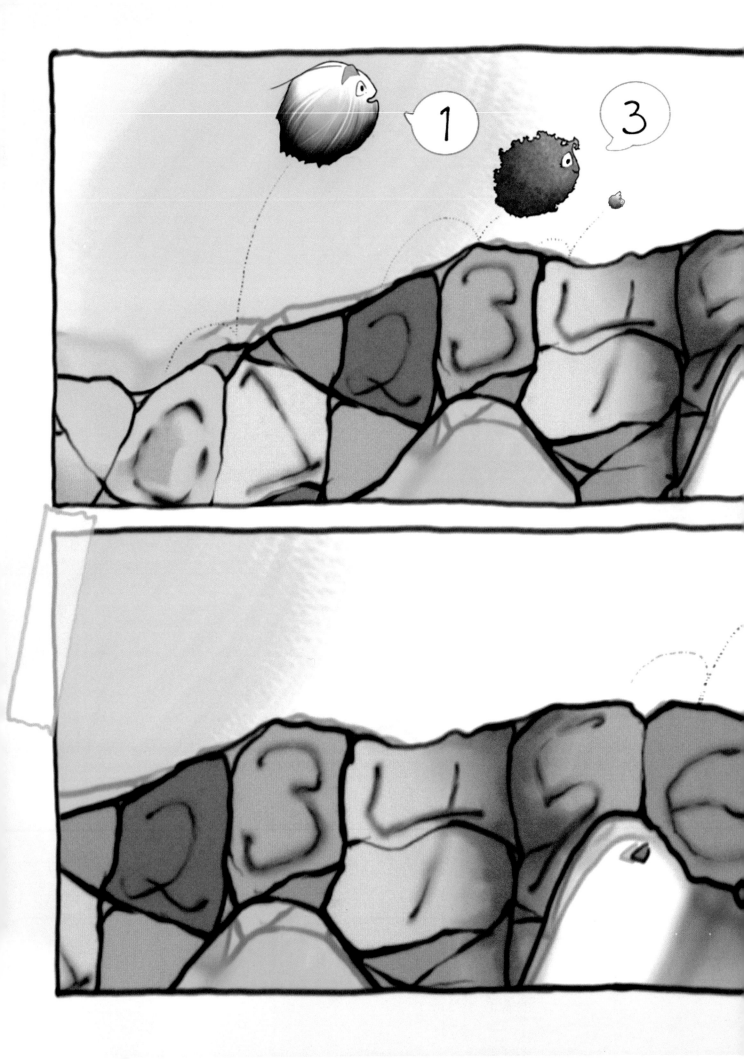

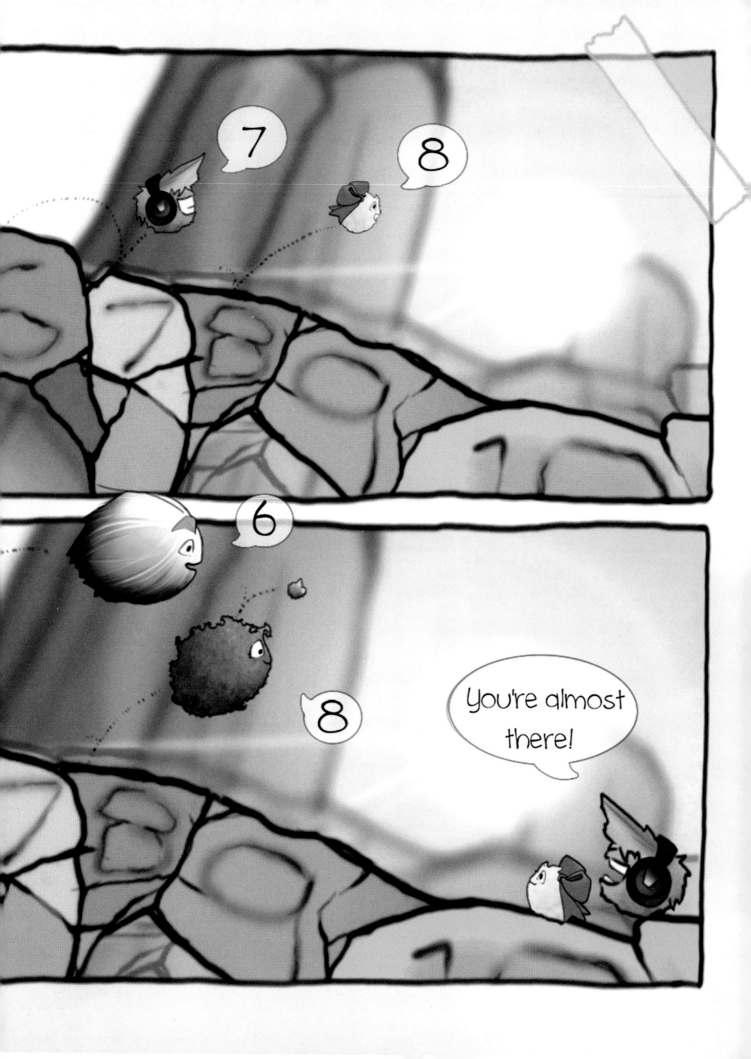

The entire Fuzzball family is thrilled to have made it across the bridge safely.
Can I get a high fur?

Everyone does the Fuzzball Happy Dance.
This just means there is a lot of jumping
and high furs... I mean high fives. However,
soon the Fuzzballs come to another bridge.

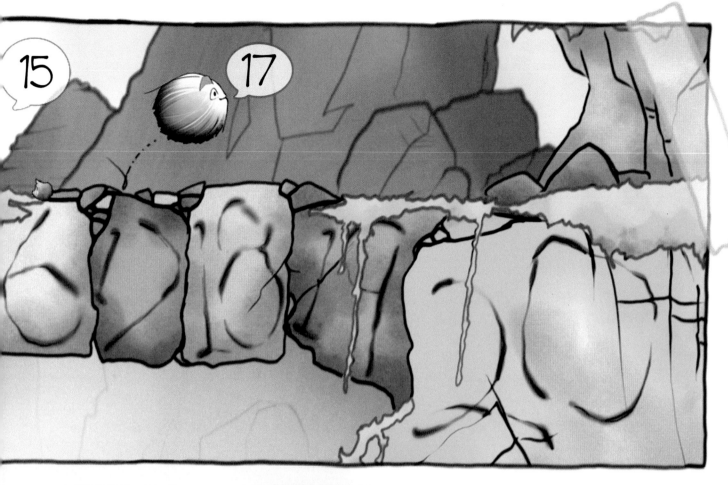

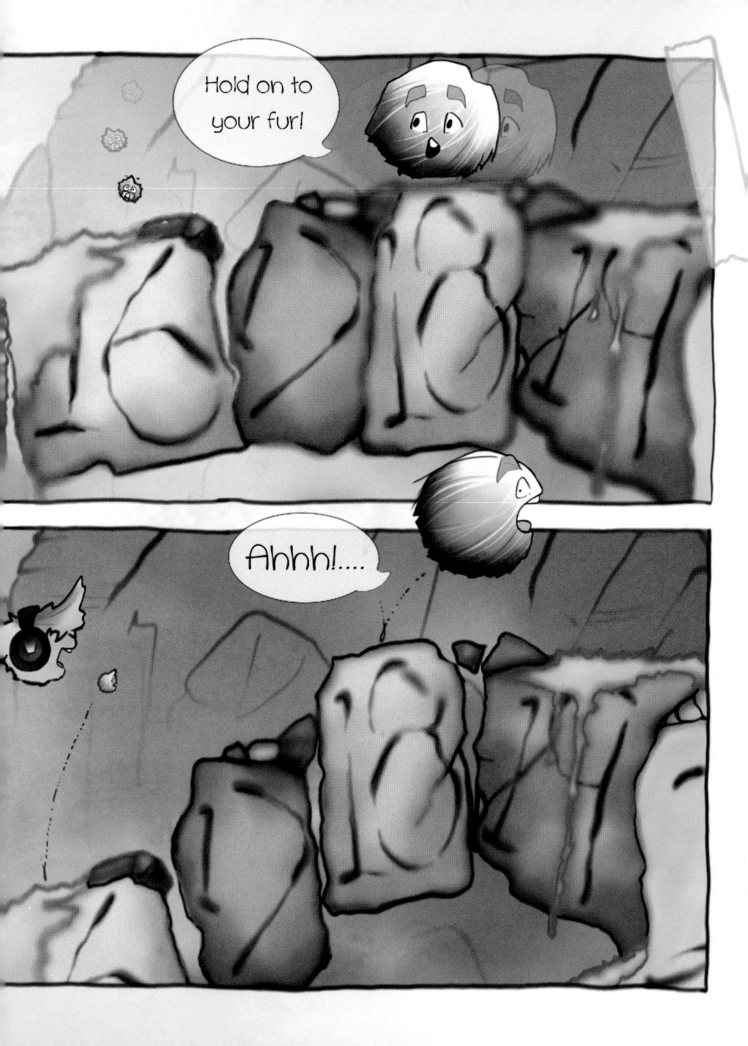

After Mama and Sister Fuzzball get over the shock of the falling bridge, Sister remembers she has packed a raft.

Once the raft is blown up Mama and Sister start the terrifying trip across the water.

As the Fuzzballs cross the final bridge, they finally see why Father had taken them on their dangerous journey.

About the
Author & Illustrator

KA Long lives and works as a
teacher in Northern Virginia.
He has a Masters in Special
Education and has been teaching
2nd grade for over 10 years.
During his own elementary years,
he frustrated many teachers with
his inability to understand simple
concepts. He now uses his unique
perspective to come up with new
and creative ways to convey
concepts to young learners in his
class. He hopes this math
tale entertains and excites
children about rounding
numbers.

Special Thanks

Before I close I must thank some very important people for this book. Thank you Ray for your support, encouragement and the technology that started this new journey. Thank you Katie, Sarah and Lisa for seeing what I was trying to create and caring enough to help make it better. Finally, thank you Jane for double checking all of my ridiculous spelling and missing commas. I love you all and could not have done this without each of you!

Sincerely,

HA Long

Made in the USA
Middletown, DE
28 September 2019